Adapted by Jasmine Jones

Based on the television series, "Lizzie McGuire", created by Terri Minsky

Part One is based on the episode written by Nina G. Bargiel & Jeremy J. Bargiel

Part Two is based on the episode written by Nina G. Bargiel & Jeremy J. Bargiel

New York

Printed in the United States of America

First Edition
1 3 5 7 9 10 8 6 4 2

Library of Congress Catalog Card Number: 2004112666

ISBN 0-7868-4682-8
For more Disney Press fun, visit www.disneybooks.com
Visit DisneyChannel.com

PART ONE

CHAPTER ONE

"**G**reat job, girls," Ms. Moran said as she watched Lizzie McGuire and Lizzie's best friend, Miranda Sanchez, pack cans of food into cardboard boxes. "This is the most successful food drive Hillridge Junior High has ever had."

"Thanks," Lizzie said brightly, tucking another can into the box. "It was actually kind of fun."

Lizzie had really enjoyed spreading the

word about homelessness and hunger to her friends and family. It made her feel like she was doing something important—like she was making a change. Plus, she and Miranda listened to music and gossiped the whole time they packed the boxes—stuff they would have been doing anyway. It was nice to *help* out and *hang* out at the same time. And, they got bonus points in Social Studies.

"The extra credit rocks," Miranda pointed out.

"You girls have a knack for this," Ms. Moran said. "You know, someone won't go hungry tonight because of all the food you collected. You two might want to think about taking on a *new* volunteer project."

Lizzie looked down at the can of beets in her hand. Someone is going to use these, she thought. It was good to know that she was helping people.

"Hey, girls!" Mr. McGuire said as he walked into the food drive. Lizzie's mother and annoying little brother Matt trailed behind him.

"Hey," Lizzie said. What's up with the reflecto-dorko gear? Lizzie wondered as she eyed her brother, who was staring dejectedly at his shoes. Of course, in Lizzie's opinion, Matt was always dressed dweebnoramously, but today he was over the top—he actually had on a bright orange belt and sash with a badge on it. Officer Pipsqueak, Lizzie thought.

"Lizzie, you forgot these cans I put out for you." Mr. McGuire handed Lizzie a brown paper bag, which was filled with food for the hungry.

Miranda wiped her hands on her jeans. "I gotta go meet my mom. Hasta la bye-bye." She gave Lizzie a quick hug and took off.

"Bye," Lizzie said, smiling as she watched her friend leave. Lizzie was glad that she and Miranda were so on the same wavelength. When it came time to do something for the world, Lizzie thought, Miranda and I just put up our hair into no-nonsense dos, slapped on our work clothes, and did some serious can-sorting. And we both loved it!

But with Matt around, Lizzie's thoughts could hardly stay on a nice topic, like saving the world.

"So," she said, turning to face Matt, "they finally came up with an official uniform for the socially challenged."

"Lizzie!" her parents chorused.

Matt put up a hand and just shook his head sadly. "No, Mom. No, Dad," he said with a sigh. "You can't be mad at her for speaking the truth."

Mrs. McGuire wrapped her hands around Matt's shoulders. "Your brother is wearing his hall monitor safety patrol belt," Mrs. McGuire announced.

Wow, Lizzie thought. Mom just said that as though she thinks it's something to be proud of.

"Hall monitor?" she repeated, scoffing. "How many garbage cans are you going to get stuck in?"

"See?" Matt whined, turning to his parents. "Even my lame-o sister knows what's coming!"

"Now, honey," Mrs. McGuire said, leaning in closely and giving Matt's shoulder a squeeze, "hall monitor is a very important job. And you should make the best of it."

"That's right, son," Mr. McGuire agreed, proudly. "It's a position of honor. I remember when I was a hall monitor. . . ."

Lizzie raised her eyebrows dubiously. What was her dad talking about? She'd heard the stories. When her dad had been chosen for hall monitor, he'd been shoved headfirst into a garbage can every day for an entire month.

Mr. McGuire stared off into space for a moment, remembering this little detail, no doubt. Finally, he had to admit the truth. "Your sister may be right, son."

Lizzie nodded. Sad but true, she thought. Oh, well. At least it's Matt who's going to suffer, and not someone I actually like!

Later that night, Lizzie shared a typical three-way call with Miranda and her other best friend, David "Gordo" Gordon.

"Gordo, why weren't you at the food drive?" Lizzie asked.

"I had something more important to do," Gordo said.

"More important than ending world hunger?" Lizzie snapped. I can't wait to hear this one, Lizzie thought, straightening her back. He probably spent the afternoon reorganizing his Frank Sinatra records, or watching obscure Japanese art films. Gordo was really sweet and smart, but he could be a little weird sometimes.

"The Science Olympics," Gordo explained. "They're this week. The long-distance paper airplane contest, the egg drop, and the ultimate test of brains and brawn . . . the slow bicycle race."

Only Gordo would put "egg drop" at the top of his priorities list.

"Uh, Gordo," Miranda said, "Tudgeman always wins those."

Lizzie nodded. Larry Tudgeman was King Nerd of Hillridge Junior High. He'd probably been working on the Science Olympics for the past twelve months—since the moment he won the last one.

"Not this year," Gordo shot back. "This year, he's goin' down."

Lizzie flopped back on her bed. "So, I guess this means you won't be recycling with us," she said.

"Uh," Miranda broke in, "when did we decide on recycling?"

Lizzie frowned. Gee, it almost sounds like Miranda isn't into the idea, Lizzie thought. But that can't be true. It's such an easy thing to do, and it could make such a difference. . . .

"Good luck with that saving the earth thing, guys," Gordo said. "I gotta go drop eggs off the roof." He clicked off.

"Hey, Miranda, meet me at the Digital Bean tomorrow," Lizzie told her only friend still on the line. "'Cause we're starting there." Lizzie turned the phone off and put it back in its cradle.

Lizzie was sure that Miranda would really get into recycling once she realized how important it was. She'd be especially excited to get started after Lizzie told her about all the Internet research she'd done. She'd learned from surfing various sites that the Earth was in serious danger!

Ozone holes, pollution, droughts, endangered animals . . . Miranda will definitely want to help, Lizzie thought. She just needs someone to give her the 411. Someone like me!

". . . So Pete Galvin was comin' out of the bathroom," Matt said as he sat behind an enormous plate of fried chicken and potatoes, ignoring his food. He was still wearing his hall monitor badge and belt, and holding his hall monitor pen—as if he were ready to write up members of the family for any infractions. "I asked him for a hall pass . . . but no go. So I wrote him up. He begged me not to. He even cried." Matt leaned toward his father, smiled, and shook his head. "You know," he said thoughtfully, tapping the ballpoint pen against his chin, "I think I want to be a mall cop when I grow up."

Mrs. McGuire gave her husband a sideways glance, but he was only paying attention to Matt.

"I knew you'd get into it, son!" Mr. McGuire said happily.

"Sorry I'm late," Lizzie said as she slid into the chair beside Matt. "I was on the phone."

"That's okay, honey," Mrs. McGuire said.

"Oh, no, no, no." Matt pointed at Lizzie, then he picked up the hall monitor citation pad that sat beside his plate. "That's *not* okay. I'm going to have to write you up." He clicked his pen and started filling out the form. "Late for dinner . . ." He ripped the page off the pad and handed it to Lizzie. "That means no dessert."

Lizzie stared at the form, and then waved the paper at her brother. "Mom, tell the geek patrol that if he touches my dessert, his citation-writing days are over."

"Mom, Dad," Matt said, looking at his parents, "back me up here?"

Mrs. McGuire shook her head. "Sorry."

Matt looked shocked. "Dad!" he wailed.

"Son, why don't you let her off with a warning?" Mr. McGuire suggested.

Matt narrowed his eyes at his sister. "You're

a troublemaker, Lizzie," he snarled, shining a small flashlight in her eyes. "I'll be watching you. I've seen your kind all my life."

Lizzie rolled her eyes. "Of course you have, Officer Wacko. I live here. Anyway," she went on, turning to her parents, "before Captain Nutjob interrupted me, I was going to say that Miranda and I decided to start a recycling project. Since the food drive was such a huge success."

Mrs. McGuire smiled. "That's wonderful, Lizzie," she said.

"We're really proud of you, sweetheart," Mr. McGuire added. "So what's the plan?"

"Well, we were thinking of starting at the Digital Bean tomorrow . . ." Lizzie started.

"Great!" Mrs. McGuire nodded approvingly.

". . . but then I thought," Lizzie went on, "wouldn't it just make perfect sense to start right here at home?"

"Oh," Mrs. McGuire said, her smile fading slightly. "Okay."

"That's, uh, wonderful," Mr. McGuire said.

"We need to start separating the garbage into plastic, paper, and glass," Lizzie explained. "We'll need three separate labeled containers and someone to drive me to the recycling center each week." Lizzie smiled brightly. Piece of cake! Lizzie thought. After all, the recycling center was only an hour away by car. Maybe we can pick up trash by the side of the road on the way. . . .

"Well, that . . ." Mrs. McGuire cleared her throat. ". . . that sounds like a lot of fun."

Lizzie beamed. See? she thought. My parents totally understand the value of the environment.

"I can't wait." Mr. McGuire's voice was flat, but Lizzie didn't even notice.

She was too busy making all of her recycling plans. Maybe she could get the entire school into it! Hey, why not? she thought. All people needed was someone to get them organized. And Lizzie was perfect for the job!

CHAPTER TWO

"I didn't know saving the earth was going to be so *smelly*," Miranda griped as she pulled a plastic bottle from the mountain of trash that had collected in the Digital Bean's garbage can. Miranda curled her lip as she held the bottle between her thumb and index finger, and dropped it delicately into the bag Lizzie had set aside for plastics.

"I know, but think how much we're helping!" Lizzie said as she dug eagerly through the trash. She couldn't believe how much her pile of recyclables had grown already. And all of this would have gone to waste, Lizzie thought, if it weren't for us. Besides, she didn't really mind getting a little dirty if she was helping the world. She'd just hoped that the bright-orange sparkly bandanna she'd used to tie back her hair was keeping some of the stink off.

Miranda glanced over at the pile of garbage she was sorting through. "There's got to be a less disgusting way we can help."

"What's disgusting is *not* recycling," Lizzie said haughtily. "I mean, *look* at this." Lizzie held up a wadded-up paper bag. "We can save a tree if we recycle this. And this," Lizzie added, holding up a plastic bottle, "this can be used—"

"To save a plastic tree?" Miranda suggested sarcastically. She was getting really sick of spending the afternoon kneeling on the floor of her favorite café picking through garbage. She should be surfing the Net at one of the Bean's computers, sipping a smoothie, and tossing the plastic cup in the *garbage* without thinking about it. The way she always did.

"No," Lizzie huffed, responding to Miranda's snide comment, "to make other plastic stuff. I mean, if we keep throwing stuff away at this rate, in fifty years, there'll be enough trash gathered up to fill the state of Texas. Twice!"

Miranda rolled her eyes. "Where do you get this stuff?"

"I read," Lizzie said defensively as she sat down at a nearby table. Lizzie had spent hours the night before downloading factoids from Earth Mama's Save the Humans Web site. They had a lot of good info.

"And these!" Lizzie continued, picking up a plastic set of six-pack rings and waving it in the air. "Do you know how many dolphins get caught in these a year because people don't cut them up!"

Miranda looked skeptical. "Are we saving dolphins, too? 'Cause I thought we were just saving the Earth."

Lizzie gaped at her friend. How can she joke about something so serious? Lizzie wondered. Doesn't she care? We're talking cute little dolphins! "Dolphins are *part* of the Earth," she told Miranda.

"Okay, fine, whatever." Miranda shrugged. "Save the planet, save the dolphins. I'm going to see if our food's ready." Miranda stalked over to the counter and picked up a tray.

"Don't get too many napkins!" Lizzie called after her, worried about wasting paper. "And get me some scissors!"

i totally rule at this saving the Earth thing.

"Thanks," Lizzie said as Miranda returned. Lizzie grabbed the scissors off Miranda's café tray and started cutting up the plastic rings.

"Aren't you going to eat your burger?" Miranda asked with her mouth full.

"After I finish saving the dolphins," Lizzie said as she snipped the rings.

Miranda lifted her eyebrows. "Well, can you at least not play with the trash while we eat?"

Just then, their fellow student, Parker McKenzie, walked up to their table, pulled up a chair, and sat down. "I think what you guys are doing is really great," she said. "Like, really."

"Wow, thanks." Lizzie smiled in surprise. She and Parker had never been tight—Lizzie was surprised that Parker even batted an eye at the fact that Lizzie was stepping up. It just goes to show, Lizzie thought, do something to show you care and people will notice.

"So many people don't even care about the environment anymore," Parker complained. "They think that the Earth is, like, this infinite resource. It's not going to last forever."

Lizzie nodded. "Totally."

Parker's eyes flicked to the tray that sat in front of Miranda, untouched by Lizzie. "Is that a burger?" she asked, poking at the wrapped sandwich on Lizzie's plate.

"Yeah," Lizzie said. "You want a bite?"

Parker curled her lip, like she was seriously grossed out. "Of your *burger*?"

"Yeah, they're really good," Miranda said through a mouthful of beef.

"How can you enjoy eating some poor dead animal?" Parker demanded.

Lizzie stared at her burger. "I never thought of it that way," she admitted.

Parker scowled at her. "Well, maybe you should, meat-eater." She stood up and stalked off.

Miranda rolled her eyes. "Can you believe how weird Parker is?"

Lizzie stared down at her burger and bit her lip. Is it my imagination, Lizzie thought, or did that thing just moo at me? "I think I just became a vegetarian."

Maybe this is a little more complicated than i thought.

Lizzie frowned at her burger. How can

something look so delicious and be so disgusting at the same time? she wondered.

"You going to eat that?" Miranda asked,
eyeing the untouched hamburger.

Lizzie shook her head, and shoved the
burger over to Miranda.

Oh, well, Lizzie thought. I may be hungry,
but at least I won't have to listen to it moo
anymore.

While the girls were discussing animal ethics
at the Bean, Gordo was sitting in the science
room at Hillridge Junior High, directly oppo-
site Larry Tudgeman. Each of them was
surrounded by thick science textbooks, and
each of them was scribbling madly in his
notebook.

"You know you can't beat me, Gordo,"
Larry said without looking up from his notes.
"I *own* the Science Olympics."

"Not this year, Tudgeman," Gordo shot back, waving his pen at his foe. "You're goin' down."

Larry sat back, surveying Gordo coolly. "Am I?" he asked in a cocky tone. "I think not. Or have you forgotten last year?" Larry stood up, stalked over to Gordo's desk, and leaned over it menacingly. "Last year . . . when your egg cracked . . . like an egg?"

Gordo winced. He remembered all right. Goopy egg oozed thickly all over, while Larry stood there smiling smugly.

Larry grinned. "And let's not forget the paper-airplane distance contest," he growled, "when you nearly blinded Mr. Lang."

The memory flashed through Gordo's mind. Gordo's paper airplane had flown wildly off course—and landed directly in Mr. Lang's eye! Gordo had been lucky not to flunk science that year.

"Oh, yeah," Larry went on, "I *gave* you the slow bike race. We'll call that pity. But face it, Gordo," Larry snarled, poking Gordo on the shoulder, "the best man won." Tudgeman gestured to himself. "*Moi.*"

Turning back to his table, Larry picked up a stack of books and started for the door.

"Tudgeman!" Gordo snapped, pointing his pen in Larry's direction.

Larry stopped in his tracks.

"You know that little voice you hear late at night?" Gordo demanded as he stepped right up to Larry. "That one in the back of your head? That one that says 'Ooh! Not good enough! Ooh! I don't think I can win!'"

Larry's confident expression flickered. Narrowing his eyes, Gordo leaned in for the kill. "That's *me*, Tudgeman!" Gordo went on. "'Cause I won't eat, I won't sleep, until I beat you. I'm already in your head, Tudgeman. I own you."

Gordo grinned in triumph as Tudgeman started to twitch.

Both of them knew—it was *on*.

CHAPTER THREE

Back at the McGuire house, Matt was flipping through the day's violations.

"Jake Charlin," Matt said, chuckling softly as he flipped through his citation pad. "I gave him three citations in one day." Matt shook his head sadly. "That kid's headed for trouble."

"Three citations?" Mr. McGuire asked as he chopped up a carrot for dinner. "I never gave *three*." Mr. McGuire sounded impressed.

"Yeah," Matt said proudly. "I checked with the other hall monitors." He grinned smugly. "It's a record."

Mrs. McGuire looked up from the vegetables she was placing in a colander. "Well, Matt, just make sure you use that power responsibly," Mrs. McGuire warned.

Matt raised an eyebrow at his mother. He didn't see how he could possibly be more responsible than he already was. . . . He didn't think that there was anything more important than upholding the supreme law of the land—the Elementary School Rules of Conduct. Matt saw himself as an instrument of justice. The short arm of the law.

Lizzie trudged in with an armful of clothes.

"What're those for?" Mrs. McGuire asked, eyeing what looked like the laundry.

Matt leaned in, flashing his minilight in Lizzie's eyes. "You better answer the question, McGuire," Matt snapped at his sister. "And it better be the truth."

Lizzie tried to shield her eyes from the glare of Matt's interrogation light. Does he really have to play psycho-cop right now? she wondered. She decided to ignore him. "Uh, Miranda and I decided to donate clothes to the homeless shelter," she told her mother. "Besides, I haven't worn this stuff in ages anyway."

Mr. McGuire looked curious. "I thought you guys were doing recycling," he said.

"Oh, we're doing that, too," Lizzie said offhandedly.

"Aren't you taking on a lot?" Mr. McGuire asked.

Lizzie blinked at him. She couldn't believe what she was hearing!

Well, if my parents' generation wasn't so interested in bell-bottoms and roller disco, the planet would be in a lot better shape!

"Dad, there's a lot to worry about!" Lizzie complained.

Mrs. McGuire started washing green beans. Lizzie put her clothes down, walked to the sink, and turned off the water. Then she grabbed a can that was lying on the counter. "Oh, and we're taking some more canned food down to the shelter," Lizzie said.

"Wait, I *need* that to make dinner," Mrs. McGuire said as she plucked the can back from Lizzie. Mrs. McGuire then turned the water back on to finish with the green beans.

Lizzie turned off the water again and grabbed the can back. "Mom, the homeless need it more than we do."

"Honey," Mr. McGuire said patiently, "we just gave the shelter a whole bunch of cans."

"Dad, the homeless population has exploded in the last five years!" Lizzie cried.

Lizzie's mother frowned at her and turned the water back on. Lizzie slammed it off. Mrs. McGuire turned it on. Lizzie turned it off. On. Off.

"What are you *doing*?" Mrs. McGuire demanded finally.

"Mom, water is a valuable resource, and the Earth does not have an infinite amount!" Lizzie snapped. It's not like every family can go around washing their vegetables in an Olympic-sized swimming pool every night! Lizzie wanted to say.

"Geekzilla's right, Mom," Matt agreed.

"Can't waste water." He scribbled on his pad. "I'm going to have to write you up."

Mrs. McGuire frowned at the citation Matt was writing up. "Fine," she snapped at Lizzie. "No clean vegetables, no dinner."

Matt thought about this for a minute, then turned back to his pad. "Delaying dinner," he explained as he handed a citation to Lizzie. "I believe that's another offense."

I'll show you offense! Lizzie thought, but before she could speak, her dad ducked into the conversation.

"Hey, Matt, why don't you let your mother and sister work this out," Mr. McGuire suggested. "Help me take out the garbage."

Lizzie looked over at the garbage. Only one bag? she thought. And plastics are sticking out of the top! Hel-lo? Hasn't anyone been listening to a word I've been saying?

"A little help here?" Lizzie griped. "Do you

realize how many trees could die because you haven't separated the paper from the plastic?"

"Okay," Lizzie's mom huffed, "I separate the laundry."

Typical mom. i'm talking about saving the world, and she's talking about laundry.

Lizzie shook her head. "I thought you'd be a little more supportive. You agreed to separate the garbage and you didn't follow through. If I did that, you'd be mad at me!"

"That's correct," Mr. McGuire said slowly, his hands planted at his waist. "But I think you need to recycle your attitude, young lady."

The doorbell rang, and Lizzie stomped off to answer it.

Miranda was standing on the doorstep—looking seriously stylin' in a brand-new baby blue leather jacket. Grinning, she spun around, so Lizzie could get a good look.

Leather! Lizzie couldn't believe her eyes. Okay, so the jacket was fabulous. But it was also *cow skin*! Ugh! "Where did you get that?" Lizzie demanded.

"At the mall," Miranda said, grinning. "Isn't it fab?"

"Miranda, you can't wear that."

Miranda gave her a What-Are-You-Talking-About look. "Are you kidding? This is totally in," Miranda said.

"But I thought we were going veggie. . . ." Lizzie said.

"Back up," Miranda commanded. "*You're* going veggie. And besides, what does that have to do with my jacket?"

"It's leather," Lizzie said, as if she were

explaining something to a six-year-old. "Leather is cow. Cow is meat. I don't eat meat."

"Fine," Miranda snapped, folding her arms across her chest. "So don't eat my jacket."

Lizzie's eyes widened. "I can't believe you. I thought you cared about the environment," she said.

"Chill," Miranda said angrily. "It's just a jacket."

"Obviously I can't count on you for help." Lizzie couldn't believe her friend. Doesn't she understand how important this is to me? Lizzie wondered. Doesn't she understand how important it is to the world? "So I'm just going to have to do this all by myself."

"Lizzie, you're totally overreacting!" Miranda said.

"I'm overreacting?" Lizzie shouted. "Tell me that I'm overreacting when the garbage builds up so high that it blocks out all the sunlight and we freeze!"

"Yeah, well at least I'll have my jacket to keep me warm!" Miranda shot back.

Miranda turned and stomped away just as Lizzie slammed the door behind her.

Lizzie rolled her eyes and leaned against the front door. "I can't believe her," Lizzie growled. She suddenly had the feeling that she was going to have to save the world all by herself.

CHAPTER FOUR

"Finally. There you are," Miranda said as she flopped into a desk beside Gordo. He had his nose buried in a book—as usual. He was surrounded by books and pieces of paper in various stages of being folded, many of which littered the ground at his feet. All prototypes for the perfect paper airplane, no doubt. He was taking this Science Olympics thing way too seriously.

"Gordo, we have to talk about Lizzie,"

Miranda said, but Gordo didn't reply. And that was when Miranda noticed he wasn't *reading* the book—he was facedown in it, fast asleep. "Gordo!" she shouted.

Gordo's eyes snapped open and he immediately started working on the paper airplane in his hand. "Can't talk," he said in a zombie voice. "Folding."

"Gordo, Lizzie's gone *loco*," Miranda explained.

"Can't talk. Still folding," Gordo replied.

"Hello?" Miranda cried. "What's wrong with you?"

Miranda was starting to think that there was something in the water. All of her friends were acting beyond weird.

"Paper airplane distance contest," Gordo said in his zombie voice. "After school. Must—" He yawned, covering his mouth, then went on, "—beat Tudgeman."

"Gordo, this is serious," Miranda said. "She's ending our friendship over a stupid leather jacket." Miranda waved her hand dismissively. "Okay, a *really cool* leather jacket. But you know what I mean."

"She'll get over it," Gordo said, only half paying attention. Then he held up his airplane and let it go. It only sailed about three feet before crashing. "Argh!" he cried in frustration.

Miranda frowned at the crumpled paper. "Is it supposed to do that?"

Suddenly, Miranda looked up and gasped. Lizzie was standing in the doorway—and she was wearing something that looked a lot like . . . a potato sack. Lizzie hurried over to her friends and quickly started collecting Gordo's rejected paper airplanes.

"What are you doing?" Gordo shouted, suddenly wide-awake as Lizzie reached for the papers on his desk. He crouched protectively over his airplanes. "I'm working on these!"

"Ninety-nine percent of all paper products are recyclable," Lizzie recited, "and yet only fifteen percent of people recycle."

Gordo thought about that for a moment. "That makes no sense."

"Exactly!" Lizzie crowed, reaching for the paper in Gordo's hands. Gordo snatched his paper airplanes out of her reach.

"I need to test out multiple designs to see which one travels the farthest," Gordo explained, trying to salvage his planes.

"Why?" Lizzie demanded.

"So I can beat Tudgeman."

Tudgeman!? Lizzie thought. *Tudgeman?!* "Beating Tudgeman is *not* more important than saving trees!" Lizzie insisted.

"This is all I've dreamed about ever since the fourth grade," Gordo said. "Recycling is going to have to wait."

"Well, saving the Earth can't wait," Lizzie said self-righteously, pounding her fist on his desk.

They both turned to Miranda for backup.

"I think I'll be eating my lunch alone today," Miranda said.

Over at his elementary school, Matt glanced at the large hall clock. Twenty seconds till the start of his shift. He slicked back his hair and tied on his neon-orange safety belt, giving his badge a quick buff. With ten seconds to go, he slipped on a large pair of aviator sunglasses, whipped out his citation pad, and gave his whistle a practice blast. Then he checked the clock again.

Showtime.

Matt flipped open his pad. "Time to go to work," he announced.

A few moments later, a blond girl sped by

on her scooter, holding her helmet under her arm. Stopping her with a blast of his whistle, Matt put the helmet on the girl's head, then pointed to a large BUCKLE UP sign, and wrote her a citation. The girl started to scoot away, but Matt pointed to another sign on the wall that read NO SCOOTERS—another citation for her.

A group of kids walked down the hallway, laughing and talking loudly. Matt stopped them, and pointed to a sign on the door of a nearby classroom. TEST IN PROGRESS the sign read. He scribbled out citations for the noisy group.

Just then, Matt spotted his teacher, Mr. Warner, trotting down the hall on his way to class. Matt held up his hand and pointed to a sign reading WALK! DON'T RUN. Matt wrote out a citation and handed it over. After all, nobody is above the law.

Mr. Warner stared down at the citation. "Surely you must be joking."

"I'm not joking," Matt said, lowering his shades. "And don't call me Shirley."

Mr. Warner grabbed Matt by the back of his orange safety belt and carried him down the hall, his legs flailing like crazy.

"Respect my authority!" Matt shouted.

Mr. Warner *did* respect his authority . . . after all, he was trying his best not to laugh.

Back at Hillridge, Gordo stood at the end of the hall, staring Tudgeman down. It was the last day of the Science Olympics. Gordo knew that if he could undermine Tudgeman's confidence, the slow bike race was his. After all, he had won it last year—he could do it again. But Tudgeman understood Gordo's game—and he was doing his best not to crack.

The two competitors were locked in an

old-fashioned stare-off . . . and the Tudge was starting to sweat.

Gordo narrowed his eyes.

Larry lifted an eyebrow, and tightened his grip on the calculator in his hand. A bead of sweat trickled down his face.

A lone tumbleweed drifted across the hallway.

Gordo tried not to wonder where the heck the tumbleweed came from as he tossed his bike helmet from hand to hand. Finally, Larry scurried away.

Smiling in satisfaction, Gordo let out a massive yawn.

"What are you doing?" Miranda asked as she walked up to Gordo.

Gordo yawned. "I was intimidating Tudgeman," Gordo explained, rolling his eyes.

"Yeah, that *yawn* looked pretty scary," Miranda said, her voice dripping with sarcasm.

"Yeah, well, it's working," Gordo replied. He and Miranda fell into step as they started toward their social studies class. "My late nights are actually paying off. We're tied. He won the egg drop, and I won the long-distance paper airplane contest. Now it all comes down to the slow bike race after school. The last person to cross the finish line wins." He let out another yawn.

Miranda cocked an eyebrow at him. "I think you need to trade that bike helmet in for a pillow." She smiled, and patted him on the shoulder. "But I'll be out there cheering you on. And I'm hoping Lizzie will be, too."

Gordo flopped at his desk the minute they reached class. He dropped his head, shut his eyes, and crashed.

"Hey!" Miranda said brightly as she sat down at the desk next to Lizzie's.

"Yes?" Lizzie huffed primly.

Biting her lip, Miranda sat fidgeting with a pencil.

"Lizzie, listen," she said gently. "I'm not wearing leather today, I didn't eat meat last night at dinner, and I recycled my soda can at lunch. So can I talk to you?"

Lizzie shrugged. "I guess."

"What are you wearing?" Miranda asked, eyeing Lizzie's all-brown, all-natural, *way*-all-*ugly* outfit. It was a pretty far cry from Lizzie's usual bright colors and sparkly accessories.

"Burlap," Lizzie snapped. "It's a renewable resource."

"Okay, Lizzie," Miranda said, shaking her head. "I'm really worried about you."

"Don't be worrying about me, Miranda," Lizzie said, her voice deadly serious. "Be worried about the world. Be worried about the environment and the homeless people and the animals and the rain forests and the ozone layer." And I don't even think I need to mention global warming, the whales, or the polar ice caps, which are melting as we speak! Lizzie added mentally.

"Well, the rain forest isn't going to hang out with me and rent movies with me on Friday nights," Miranda said. "Can't you just put this aside for a few hours? Let's go watch Gordo at the slow bike race after school," she pleaded.

Just then, Ms. Moran walked into the room. "Okay, everyone," she announced, "clear your desk for a pop quiz."

Everyone began to clear their desks. Well, everyone, that is, but Gordo. His head was still down on his desk, and he was snoring softly.

"Mr. Gordon?" Ms. Moran prompted. "Are you still with us?"

Gordo's eyes fluttered open blearily. "I'm

just resting my eyes," he insisted, then plopped his head back onto his desk.

Ms. Moran began to hand out the two-page quiz. Lizzie frowned as she took a quiz from the person in front of her. "Ms. Moran?" she shouted.

"Lizzie, don't . . ." Miranda whispered. She knew what was coming.

"Lizzie, there'll be time for your question after the quiz," Ms. Moran said.

Lizzie stood up. "No, there won't be time!"

"Lizzie!" Miranda pleaded. She knew where this was headed—and it definitely wasn't going to help Lizzie's social studies grade. "Don't."

"Ms. Moran, we're running out of time!" Lizzie insisted.

The teacher's eyes widened. "Lizzie," she said, "quiet."

"I won't be quiet!" Lizzie huffed.

Miranda put her head in her hands. "Here we go."

"Do you know how many trees you killed with your little quiz?" Lizzie demanded, getting right into Ms. Moran's face. "You could've printed those double-sided! You could've saved a life!"

Tree-killer!

"I'm going to ask you one last time, Lizzie, to sit down and be quiet." Ms. Moran's voice was low and her eyes flashed dangerously. "We'll discuss this after the quiz."

"I would expect you out of all people to understand!" Lizzie said, her hands planted on her hips. "You encouraged us to start this project! Why won't anyone help me?"

"Ms. McGuire, I'm going to help you," Ms. Moran said. "I am sending you home to get some sleep."

That's not good.

Ms. Moran handed Lizzie a hall pass. Lizzie blinked at it for a moment. Omigosh, she thought as she took the bright orange pass from her teacher. What have I done? Not only was she in serious trouble—but Ms. Moran had just used up yet *another* piece of paper . . . and it was all Lizzie's fault!

Lizzie walked out of the classroom, shutting the door behind her.

"I'm not sleeping!" Gordo insisted, his eyes snapping open at the sound of the door. "Just resting my eyes."

CHAPTER FIVE

"**H**ey," Mrs. McGuire said as Lizzie trudged into the kitchen. She glanced at her watch in confusion. "Is it 3:00 already?" Matt and Mr. McGuire were sitting at the kitchen table, and Lizzie's mom was fixing everyone a snack.

"No," Lizzie admitted. "I got sent home early."

"I got sent home early, too," Matt griped. "They said I was power-hungry. I don't even know what that means, but I've got to get back to school." His eyes were wide as he pounded the table in frustration.

"Son," Mr. McGuire said gently, "you have to know when it's time to turn in your belt."

"But I can't leave my post!" Matt wailed.

"Honey, the school will be fine," his mom assured him. "You need to take a rest."

"I'm sure there are other hall monitors on duty," Mr. McGuire added.

"But I'm the best!" Matt said desperately, falling face-first into his snack plate.

Mrs. McGuire gave Matt a stern look. "We'll talk about it later. Matt, get out of your sandwich."

Lizzie stared at her brother. "Okay, now he is scary."

"*He's* scary?" Mrs. McGuire looked at Lizzie over the top of her glasses.

"Lizzie, I hate to break this to you," Mr.

McGuire said gently, "but you two have more in common than you think."

"Lizzie," Mrs. McGuire said as she led her daughter into the living room, "you've got a big heart, and we're very proud of you."

"But you're taking on too much," her father said. "You can't save the world by yourself."

"Well, no one else is helping," Lizzie complained, throwing herself on the couch.

"Well, okay." Mr. McGuire looked thoughtful. "We're going to help. Recycling garbage, that's a very good idea."

"Yeah, and we're going to be a lot better about that," Mrs. McGuire chimed in. "But you've got to relax."

Lizzie shook her head. "How can I relax?"

"Lizzie, honey, you're running yourself into the ground," Mrs. McGuire said.

Mr. McGuire nodded as both he and his wife sat down next to Lizzie. "You can't get anything done if you can't take care of your-self first."

Lizzie hesitated. "I never thought of it that way."

"Well, if you really want to make a differ-ence, what you have to do is pick one thing," Mr. McGuire told her, putting his arm around her shoulders, "just one thing and go for it."

One thing? Lizzie thought. How can I pick just one thing when there are so many things wrong with the world?

"And get some help, too," Mrs. McGuire suggested. "I mean, what happened to Gordo and Miranda?"

Lizzie sighed. "Well, I was kind of a jerk," she admitted. Kind of a jerk? Lizzie thought. That's putting it too mildly. "No, you know what?" Lizzie said. "I was a *big* jerk. Can I go back to school and watch Gordo win the slow bicycle race?"

Mrs. McGuire nodded. "I'll tell you what. You go take a nap, and I'll wake you up and I'll drive you back up to school later."

"You get upstairs right now and get some sleep," Mr. McGuire said.

Lizzie winced. "Um," she said sheepishly. "I can't."

Lizzie's mother looked confused. "Why not?"

"Well," Lizzie hedged. "I kind of donated my mattress to the homeless shelter." She gave her parents an uncomfortable grin.

Mrs. McGuire sighed. "I'll go get a blanket for the couch."

"I'll call the shelter," Mr. McGuire said, heading for the phone.

Lizzie smiled as she watched her parents leap into action. It felt good to let somebody else take care of things for a change.

CHAPTER SIX

Lizzie and Miranda stood at the edge of the track that had been set up around the edge of the quad for the slow bike race. They were both clapping like crazy. I know Gordo is going to win this thing, Lizzie thought eagerly. He's been working so hard—he *has* to win!

"Ladies and gentlemen," the announcer's voice blared over the loudspeaker, "we've come to the slow-speed bicycle race. And now presenting last year's overall champion, Larry Tudgeman."

Larry stepped before the crowd, which erupted into boos. Sneering, Larry flipped the enormous purple cape he was wearing and mounted his bike.

"And here, Mr. David 'Gordo' Gordon!" the announcer said as Gordo trotted down the stairs to the quadrangle.

The crowd went wild. Gordo's outfit was a showstopper—a white rhinestone Elvis-style jumpsuit with batwings under the arms and enormous, wind-grabbing bell-bottoms. His huge white collar extended past his head— halfway up the combination enormous bouffant wig and bike helmet he wore. Turning, Gordo struck a pose, showing off the back of his jumpsuit—where "Gordo" was spelled out in rhinestones.

No wonder he hasn't been getting any

sleep, Lizzie thought as Gordo walked to his bike, and the crowd went wild. He's spending all his late nights learning to sew!

"Move your bicycles to the start/finish line and get ready to bicycle!" the announcer called.

"Wow," Miranda said as she and Lizzie joined Gordo at the starting line.

"Very cool," Lizzie agreed. That's something I never thought I'd say at a Science Olympics, Lizzie thought, eyeing Gordo's outfit.

"And it's aerodynamically designed to increase my wind resistance and slow me down," Gordo added.

Hmm, Lizzie thought. Well, it's still cool. "Good luck," she said as she and Miranda stepped back into the crowd.

Larry turned to Gordo and frowned. "Who are you?"

"I'm the King, baby," Gordo said in his best Elvis voice.

"The race will be once around the quad," the announcer's voice boomed over the PA. "Riding only. No standing. No walking. No leaning. Last bicycle across the finish line is the winner."

Larry and Gordo leaned over their handlebars, ready for action. A moment later, the whistle blew, and the race was on.

For the first few seconds, Larry and Gordo were neck and neck. But almost immediately, against his will, Larry pulled ahead.

"And they're off!" the announcer shouted. "Tudgeman takes an early lead and Gordo settles in behind him."

The crowd went wild as Gordo hung back, still upright, still moving at a snail's pace. The crowd started to chant his name, "Gor-do! Gor-do! Gor-do!"

Gordo fell even further behind—he was mind-bogglingly slow! He was a lock to win!

Gordo had to stifle a yawn . . . he didn't have much farther to go. . . .

"GOR-DO! GOR-DO! GOR-DO!"

"Coming down the backstretch, Gordo is increasing his deficit," the announcer narrated. "Tudgeman just can't seem to hold back. It's going to take more than wind resistance to help Tudgeman today. Gordo's making it look easy. Whoa, Gordo drops further behind as Tudgeman heads into the last turn. If Tudgeman crosses, he loses."

Cross the line! Lizzie thought frantically. Cross the line, Tudgeman!

"Tudgeman's run out of real estate," the announcer went on. "Gordo's going to win this thing. Two feet. One foot. Six inches."

Suddenly, Gordo's bike hesitated, then stopped. His eyelids fluttered, and he let out an enormous yawn. His bouffant wig drooped over his eyes.

Oh, no! Lizzie thought as she watched in horror. Gordo's falling asleep!

Gordo's bike wobbled, and then toppled to the ground.

"And Gordo's disqualified for leaving his bike!" the announcer barked. "Tudgeman wins by default!"

Lizzie and Miranda rushed over to their fallen friend.

"Are you okay?" Lizzie asked.

Miranda stared down at Gordo, who was sprawled out over the red bricks of the quad. "Yeah, Gordo, you went down pretty hard," she said.

"Thank you," Gordo said, Elvis-like. "Thankyouverymuch." Then he fell asleep again.

Miranda looked at Lizzie. "Gordo has left the building."

CHAPTER SEVEN

It took a while for Gordo to wake up, but when he did, the girls offered to walk home with him. They had to go pretty slowly, given Gordo's wind-resistant outfit and the bent wheel on his bicycle.

"Let me be the first to say, I was a total jerk," Lizzie said, giving her friends a sheepish look. "And I'm really sorry."

"Good," Miranda said. "You should be." Then she gave Lizzie a tiny smile. "But you were kind of right. So, I'm making my family cut up those six-pack rings, because I like dolphins."

"I'm really sorry you didn't win the race, Gordo," Lizzie said.

"Yeah," Gordo said with a sigh, "me too. If I hadn't stayed up all night creating my aero-dynamic collar, I wouldn't have fallen asleep. I might have won." He blinked. "There's probably a lesson in there somewhere, but I'm just too tired to find it."

Miranda grinned. "At least you were stylin'."

"And there's always next year," Lizzie added.

"And you," Miranda said to Lizzie, "please tell me your days of burlap chic are over."

"They are," Lizzie promised, looking down at her outfit. She was wearing a typical-Lizzie-style blue paisley top, and red pants. "I think

I'm just going to pick one thing and stick to it." She thought for a moment. "Like stray dogs. Do you know how many dogs are abandoned at shelters each year?"

Miranda and Gordo rolled their eyes.

Well, so what if it's a new cause? Lizzie thought. Dogs are cute! And I could totally save a few by keeping them in the backyard. . . .

Can i keep them, Mom? Can i?

"Oh, look!" Larry said as he rode by. "The aliens brought Elvis back! And they shrunk him!" Larry cackled madly and rode off, sneering over his shoulder.

"I hate that guy!" Gordo snarled.

"Hey, Larry!" Lizzie called. "Look out for that—"

Lizzie winced as Larry took a nosedive into a garbage can, and Tudgeman and the garbage went spilling all over the street.

"Never mind!" Miranda shouted.

"It's okay!" Larry called weakly. "It's okay. I'm good."

Cracking up, the three friends headed home. For the first time in weeks, Lizzie wasn't angry to see garbage in the street! Tudgeman was down for the count, Gordo was back to his same old self, and Lizzie was happy to be through with her burlap phase. Everything was great. Just like it should be. Back to *normal*.

Now, about those stray dogs . . .

**PART
TWO**

CHAPTER ONE

"Okay," Lizzie said into her phone. "I'll see you guys soon." She nodded, giggling. "Yeah." Lizzie said good-bye and turned her cordless phone off. She had been talking to her two best friends, David "Gordo" Gordon and Miranda Sanchez. Once the three of them got rolling on a good conversation, it was kind of hard to stop.

"Nice of you to join us," Mrs. McGuire said sarcastically as Lizzie set down the phone.

"It's not that nice," Lizzie's annoying little brother, Matt, said.

Lizzie rolled her eyes and ignored him.

"Sam," Mrs. McGuire shouted to her husband, "come on! Your lunch is getting cold!" she said as she spooned out some of her famous vegetable soup.

Mr. McGuire trotted into the kitchen. Oh, no, Lizzie thought as she eyed her dad's outfit. This is what happens when Mom doesn't help Dad get dressed in the morning.

Mr. McGuire was wearing a football jersey, a baseball cap, an orange sports vest, and a giant foam Number One hand.

"We don't have time for lunch!" Mr. McGuire insisted, waving his foam hand frantically. "We can grab lunch on the way."

Mrs. McGuire raised her eyebrows. "On the way to *what*?"

"The Super Sports Expo!" Mr. McGuire

cried. "Come on, you promised you'd go." He poked his wife in the shoulder with a foam finger.

Mrs. McGuire ducked away from the giant hand, looking skeptical. "Are you sure? Because that doesn't sound like something I would do."

Lizzie couldn't help smirking. At least I don't have to go to the sports expo! she thought happily. Poor Mom, though. She'll be stuck with Dad while he runs around, inspecting baseball cards and sweaty old jerseys that famous sports guys had the sense to toss out.

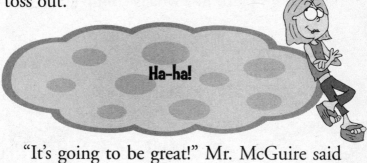

Ha-ha!

"It's going to be great!" Mr. McGuire said

enthusiastically. "They've, they've got football jerseys, they've got baseball cards . . . and last year they even had a pair of Shaq's old shoes!" Clearly unable to contain himself any longer, Mr. McGuire dashed out the front door to start the car.

"Sounds fun," Lizzie said to her mom sarcastically. Better you than me, she thought.

Mrs. McGuire put her head in her hands. It looked like she had just been hit with a supersized migraine. "Lizzie?" she asked.

Uh-oh, Lizzie thought. Something about the way she just said my name tells me that I'm not going to like what's coming. . . .

Run!

Lizzie paused with her soupspoon halfway to her mouth. "What?" she asked, her eyes wide.

"I need you to watch Matt this afternoon," Mrs. McGuire said.

Noooooooooooooooooo! Lizzie thought.

"Lanny's coming over," Matt pointed out.

"I need you to watch Matt *and* Lanny this afternoon," Mrs. McGuire corrected.

Lizzie's jaw dropped in horror.

"Mom, Mom," Lizzie said, thinking fast, "don't you think that Matt and Lanny are incredibly mature for their age?" She patted Matt on the back. "I mean, they can stay home alone."

"No," Mrs. McGuire replied flatly.

Matt shook his head. "You knew that wasn't going to work," he said to Lizzie.

"But I have plans!" Lizzie wailed. "That is so unfair."

Mrs. McGuire sighed. "Well, your plans have changed."

> **Why do i even bother making plans? i obviously exist just to watch Matt.**

"Jo McGuire!" Mr. McGuire shouted to his wife as he burst back into the kitchen, madly waving his foam hand and a pennant. "Let's go!"

Mrs. McGuire sighed again.

Okay, Lizzie said to herself as she looked at her mother, I have to admit that things *could* be worse.

Lizzie flopped on the couch beside Matt and Lanny while her father dusted off his prized possession—an autographed Walter Payton football—that sat on the mantel. He had run back inside just to see it and say good-bye before he left. Bizarre-o, Lizzie thought.

"I almost forgot," Mr. McGuire told the football. "We're going to the Super Sports Expo today. You remember the Super Sports Expo, right? That's where I found you." He patted the ball affectionately.

Lizzie rolled her eyes. She remembered when her dad had bought the football—he'd brought it home in a baby blanket. "Mom," Lizzie griped, "Dad is talking to the football again." He has more heart-to-hearts with that thing than he does with me, Lizzie thought.

"Lizzie, Lizzie, Lizzie, that isn't just a football," her dad said, planting his hands at his waist. "That's an authentic 1986 Super Bowl football signed by Walter Payton. It's my favorite thing in the whole world."

Mrs. McGuire flashed a glare at her husband, and Lizzie scoffed.

"Except for you guys, of course," Lizzie's dad added quickly.

Whatever, Lizzie thought. At least he didn't tell me to apologize to the ball.

"Honey, the car's idling," Mr. McGuire said as he hurried out the door.

"Okay," Mrs. McGuire said to the kids. "Lizzie's in charge, stay in the house, and we'll be back in a couple of hours. There's money in the kitchen for pizza."

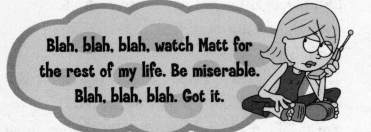

Lizzie clenched her jaw in frustration.

"Lizzie?" Mrs. McGuire said.

"This is so unfair," Lizzie grumbled.

"Sometimes life isn't fair," Lizzie's mom pointed out sadly.

"Super Sports Expo!" Mr. McGuire chanted. "Super Sports Expo! Super Sports Expo!"

Mrs. McGuire stared after her husband. "Like right now." Shaking her head, Lizzie's mom walked toward the front door.

The minute her parents were gone, Lizzie jumped off the couch to face Matt and Lanny. "Okay," she snapped, "here are the *real* ground rules. Don't bug me. And when my friends come over? Don't bug me. If you get your little head stuck in the toilet," she added, pointing to Lanny, "don't bug me. Got it?"

Lanny gave Matt a nervous look. "Don't worry, Lanny," Matt said, patting his friend on the arm. "I mean, what are the odds of you getting your head stuck in the toilet . . . again?"

Lizzie turned to storm away, and Matt stuck out his foot, tripping her. She flailed, then recovered.

"Worm," Lizzie growled.

Matt grinned at Lanny. "We got her good that time."

Shaking her fist at Matt, Lizzie stomped up to her room. I already know that this is going to be the worst day ever, she thought. Do I really have to bother living through it? Can't I just skip ahead to tomorrow?

"Four-two! Hut, hut! Hut!" Matt dropped back to the edge of the McGuire backyard, while Lanny went long for the pass. "McGuire drops back!" Matt narrated. "He starts to scramble!"

Dodging several imaginary opponents, Lanny made his way toward the other end of the yard.

"He sees Lanny breaking for the end zone!" Matt went on. "He throws as he's going down!"

Chucking the football, Matt went down hard on the green lawn, pretending to have been tackled by five large guys. The football arced through the air. It went higher . . . higher. . . . Pouring on the speed, Lanny dashed after it.

But the ball didn't come down. It was stuck in a tree.

Lanny stared up at the tree.

Matt got up and brushed himself off. "Lanny, you were covered!" Matt cried as he walked up to his friend. "I had to throw the ball away or else it would have been intercepted."

Lanny blinked calmly at Matt, then turned back to the tree. The football was stuck in a high branch. It didn't look like there was any way to get it down.

"Oops," Matt said.

CHAPTER TWO

Lizzie was at the kitchen island, studying, when Matt and Lanny walked toward the back deck carrying the Walter Payton football.

"What are you guys doing?" Lizzie demanded.

Lanny glanced nervously at Matt, and tried to hide the football. "Um, not bugging you?" Matt suggested. He and Lanny had spent at least twenty minutes shaking the tree, then tossing a Frisbee at the ball stuck in the branch, but it was no good. The football seemed to be stuck permanently. So they had done the only reasonable thing—they'd picked up the only other football in the house.

"Listen, Tweedledumb and Tweedledumber," Lizzie snapped, grabbing the football. "This right here, it's not a toy. This is one of Dad's most prized possessions, okay? And if something happens to it, that would bug me." She glared at them, waiting for her words to sink in. "Got it?"

My parents aren't paid enough to do this job.

"I'm going to go and put this in a safe place," Lizzie said. Wow, I totally just saved the day on that one, Lizzie thought as she headed toward the front hallway.

Matt and Lanny exchanged glances. "You're right, Lanny," Matt said. "She does take after my mom."

". . . Matt and Lanny were messing around with my dad's autographed football," Lizzie explained into the phone, "so I had to hide it in the hall closet for safekeeping." She was talking to Gordo, who was on a pay phone. He was studying with Miranda at the library. And I should be *with* them, Lizzie thought grumpily.

"You mean the authentic 1986 Super Bowl football signed by Walter Payton?" Gordo asked eagerly.

Lizzie rolled her eyes. Why is it that boys care about this stuff? she wondered. "No, Gordo," she said sarcastically, "the other one."

"You have *two*?" Gordo squealed.

"Put Miranda back on the phone," Lizzie snapped.

"Lizzie wants to talk to you," Gordo told Miranda.

"Hey," Miranda said. "We're just going to grab a couple of books and we'll be over soon. Okay?"

The sooner the better, Lizzie thought. "Sounds good."

"All right."

Crash!

Something horrible has just happened in the hallway, Lizzie thought as she pressed the OFF button and dashed toward the noise. I just hope I don't have to murder anybody over this. . . .

Matt and Lanny were frozen—standing in front of the downstairs hall closet. Matt was holding a game of Chinese checkers, staring at a bunch of junk at his feet. Junk that had been, only moments ago, crammed at the top of the hall closet. Junk that included . . . the Walter Payton football!

"We were getting a board game off the top shelf in the closet and all this stuff came down!" Matt wailed, his eyes wide.

Lizzie stared at the floor at the foot of the closet, where the autographed football lay wobbling. Wobbling, but safe.

Lizzie heaved a sigh of relief. "At least the football is okay."

Just then, almost as though it had heard Lizzie, her dad's bowling ball began to slowly roll off the top shelf.

"No, no, no, no, no!" Lizzie cried. But it was no use. Lizzie watched in horror as the bowling ball slipped off the edge and landed on the football with a horrible pop and a hiss.

Lizzie gaped at the ball. For a moment, she

couldn't even force herself to move. She was frozen in shock.

Go back! Do over! Rewind!

"This is not happening!" Lizzie wailed as she picked up the football. It was as flat as a steamrolled pancake and torn along one side. It's dead! Lizzie thought. "Matt!" she shouted. "Matt! You killed the football."

Matt gaped at her in horror. "I didn't kill the football!" he insisted, and Lanny nodded. "It was an accident! We didn't mean to!"

This is all Matt's fault but I'm the one who's going to get in trouble! Lizzie thought. I'm *always* the one who gets in trouble! "Matt, if you needed to get the game and you couldn't reach it, why didn't you just call for me to help you?" she wailed.

"Because you told us not to bug you," Matt said meekly.

Lizzie sighed.

Great. Now he remembers.

"We are so busted," Lizzie raged. "We're going to be grounded forever, and it's your fault! Once again, Matt, you've found a way to ruin my life. Thanks a lot. You two just go upstairs, okay? And stay there."

Matt and Lanny looked so sad as they trudged upstairs that Lizzie almost felt sorry for them.

Almost.

But she was too busy feeling sorry for herself.

* * *

"The bowling ball fell," Lizzie explained to Miranda and Gordo once her two friends arrived at the McGuire house, "the football exploded, and my life was officially over." They were seated at the kitchen table, and Lizzie was slumped in her chair.

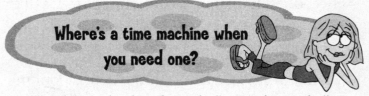

Where's a time machine when you need one?

"Look on the bright side," Gordo said. "At least your parents will never force you to watch Matt again."

"Not helping, Gordo," Lizzie snapped.

"Well," Miranda suggested carefully, "maybe it's not as bad as you think. Can you fix the ball?"

Lizzie thought for a moment. "I don't know. Can I do that?" She turned to Gordo. "Can you fix a football?"

Gordo shrugged. "I don't know, but I'm sure it can't get any worse."

"Where's the football?" Miranda asked.

"Follow me." Lizzie led her friends to the hall closet. She hadn't even had the heart to clean up the mess on the floor. What difference does it make? Lizzie thought. It's like rearranging deck chairs on the *Titanic*. I'm still going down. . . .

She rummaged through the debris, looking for the football. Not there. "Okay, it has to be in here," Lizzie said, flipping through the clothes on the rack. "Footballs don't just get up and walk away."

"Not crushed ones, anyway," Gordo cracked.

Miranda gave him a gentle whack on the arm. "Not helping, Gordo," Miranda snapped, folding her arms across her chest.

Lizzie's eyes went wide as the simple, horrifying truth hit her. "Matt." She stepped over the rubble on the floor and shouted up the stairs. "Matt, you give me that football right now!" Lizzie stormed up the stairs and shoved open the door to Matt's room. ". . . Or else you're—" But Matt wasn't there. Neither was Lanny. Neither was the football. "—gone?"

Spotting a note on Matt's desk, Miranda read aloud, " 'We went to go fix the football. We're really sorry.' And it's signed 'Matt and Lanny,' " she added, looking up at Lizzie.

"Great." Lizzie sighed, sticking her thumbs into the front pockets of her jeans. "Like I'm not in enough trouble as it is."

My little brother and his friend are missing, we killed my dad's prized possession, and i have an English test tomorrow. Things couldn't be better.

"Remember how I said it couldn't get any worse?" Gordo asked gently.

Miranda and Lizzie looked at him.

"I was wrong," Gordo admitted.

"Not helping, Gordo!" Lizzie and Miranda chorused.

Miranda slapped the note back on the desk and headed for the door.

"Come on!" Lizzie growled at Gordo as she followed Miranda. They had to get out of there. She needed a plan to find Matt and Lanny—fast.

CHAPTER THREE

"**T**hat's it," Lizzie said as she hung up the phone. "I've called all of their friends, nobody has seen or heard from Matt and Lanny."

Not that anybody would be likely to hear from Lanny, Lizzie thought. He never said a word! But still . . .

The only thing that's worse than having Matt and Lanny around is not having Matt and Lanny around!

This is turning into a major problem, Lizzie thought. "I'm going to be in so much trouble," she said.

"Why don't we just go out and look for them?" Gordo suggested.

"Yeah," Miranda agreed, nodding. "I mean, how far can two kids with a broken football go?"

"I know," Lizzie said, "but my parents are going to be home soon, you guys. We don't have time to find them and then get back."

At that moment, the phone rang. Grabbing it, Lizzie pressed the ON button and hopped out of her chair. "Matt?" she said hopefully into the receiver.

"Lizzie?" It was her mother's voice.

That was so *not* smooth, Lizzie thought. "Mom?" she asked.

Miranda pursed her lips, and Lizzie winced. Cover, McGuire, she told herself. Cover like the wind!

"Is everything okay?" Mrs. McGuire sounded worried.

it really depends on your definition of okay.

"Yeah," Lizzie said quickly. "Everything, everything is fine."

"Is Matt behaving?" Mrs. McGuire asked.

They're behaving—behaving horribly! Lizzie thought. But she couldn't really explain the whole situation to her mother. "Yeah, Matt and Lanny are great," Lizzie lied. "They're playing quietly upstairs."

Miranda and Gordo gave Lizzie a skeptical look, and Lizzie bit her lip. Ooh, that was such a bad lie, she thought. What was I thinking? Mom will never believe that one.

"Well, here's the deal," Mrs. McGuire said.

"Your dad and I are going to be a little late. 'Cause we got a flat."

"Oh, that's great!" Lizzie cried, then realized her mistake. "I mean, that's greatly . . . bad."

"So we'll be home in a couple of hours," Mrs. McGuire went on.

She sounds suspicious, Lizzie thought. I know she's onto me!

"Oh, okay," Lizzie said as nonchalantly as possible, "well, you guys just take your time. You don't get out enough as it is. I've got everything totally under control."

Miranda winced as Lizzie floundered with her story. Lizzie was the world's worst liar.

"We'll see you guys soon," Mrs. McGuire said.

"Okay," Lizzie said as she hung up the phone. "Yes!" she hissed, grinning at her friends. "Okay, we just bought some time."

She pulled a stool up to the kitchen island. "Here's the plan, guys." Lizzie pointed to Gordo and slid the phone toward him. "Okay, you're going to stay here and man the phone."

"Oh, come on," Gordo griped. "I never get to do any of the cool stuff! I want to go with you guys."

"Gordo, Matt and Lanny like you," Lizzie said reasonably. "If they call, you can convince them to come back home."

"Fine," Gordo grumbled. "Can I order a pizza?"

Lizzie rolled her eyes.

Miranda gaped at him. "Gordo, Matt and Lanny are missing, Lizzie's about to be grounded for life, and all you can think about is food?"

"I'm hungry," Gordo pointed out.

Lizzie sighed. She knew that Gordo was

completely useless when he hadn't been fed. "Fine, Gordo, order a pizza for yourself, okay." She turned to Miranda. "Miranda, you're going to come with me."

Miranda smiled. "Cool."

"Everybody clear on the plan?" Lizzie asked.

The friends nodded at one another.

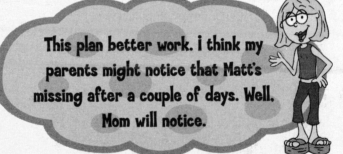

This plan better work. i think my parents might notice that Matt's missing after a couple of days. Well, Mom will notice.

"Go, go, go!" Lizzie said as her friends leaped into action.

Meanwhile, Matt and Lanny were looking for a way to raise the dead . . . the dead football, that is. Their first stop was the bike-repair shop. Matt showed the football to a woman standing among the racks and racks of bicycles. She attached the football to a hand pump to try to fill the football with air. But the ball didn't seem to be inflating. Matt grabbed the pump. He lifted and lowered the bar faster and faster. Still, the ball didn't budge. Finally, the big-muscled owner of the bike shop came over. He pumped madly, but it was no use. The air just swooshed right out of the huge tear on the side. Dejected, Matt and Lanny left to try to look for another miracle worker.

Matt suggested that they go to a magician, but Lanny thought that was lame, so their next stop was at a doctor's office. The football laid under a sheet as the doctor—an older gentleman with glasses—walked into the examining room. But when Matt pulled back the sheet to reveal the football, the doctor chased them out of his office.

Next up, Matt and Lanny tried a taxidermist. Matt stared at the stuffed and mounted animals. They were kind of freaky. After a while, the taxidermist handed back the football, which now had a creepy pair of glass eyes, horns, and, at the tear in the side, little teeth. Matt and Lanny gaped at each other. Grabbing the horns and ripping them off the football, Matt and Lanny got out of there in a hurry.

As the friends trudged through the park, they stumbled upon a rabbi and a priest playing chess. Matt sighed, thinking that maybe they really did need a miracle after all. Wordlessly, he handed the football to the rabbi.

"This is a Walter Payton autographed football!" the rabbi said. He looked at Matt and

Lanny's guilty faces, then shook his head. "You boys are in a lot of trouble."

The rabbi handed the ball to the priest, who looked at the football, then looked up at Matt, his face serious. "Sorry, son," the priest said gently, "I think he's passed."

Lanny crossed himself.

"You mean there's nothing we can do?" Matt asked.

"Only a miracle can help you now," the priest said, returning the ball to Matt.

The rabbi shrugged. "Of course, you could just replace it."

Matt's face lit up. "That's brilliant!" Lanny looked at him. "You read my mind, Lanny! We're off to Collector's Corner!" He turned back to the rabbi. "Shalom!" he shouted.

Waving, Matt and Lanny dashed off.

Finally—they seemed to have a prayer of saving the football.

CHAPTER FOUR

Gordo flopped onto the couch. "Once again, Gordo, the responsible one, gets left behind," he griped to himself. "Lizzie and Miranda get to go out and track down Matt and Lanny, while I'm here by myself." He looked around. "All alone . . ." He thought a moment, then picked up the remote that was lying in his lap. ". . . with cable . . ." he continued slowly, ". . . and video games . . . and a refrigerator full of food!" Suddenly, Gordo realized something—he was totally set up.

"For a smart guy, I can be kind of dumb sometimes."

Hopping off the couch, Gordo hurried to the kitchen. Yanking open the fridge, he pulled out some salami, turkey, pimento loaf, baloney, ham, cheddar, provolone, mayo, jelly, mustard, onions, lettuce, tomatoes, and bread. Then Gordo tackled his sandwich project. This one would be bigger and better than any sandwich that had come before.

Gordo slapped some mayo and mustard on the bread, then laid a firm foundation of cold cuts. He topped it with a little jelly, then squirted some whipped cream on top. Then another piece of bread, then some pimento loaf. Another layer of meat, and Gordo decided it was time for chocolate sauce, reasoning that it was downright wasteful to have two meals—lunch and dessert—at separate times. When he was finished, Gordo stood back to admire his creation. It was over three feet tall, and a thing of beauty. Gordo tried to wrap his hands around the sandwich, but they weren't big enough. He picked up the plate and opened his mouth, but there was no way to get a bite. He tried one angle, then another—no use. Gordo couldn't figure out how to get a grip on his lunch.

Shrugging, Gordo put down the plate. "I think I will order a pizza," he decided.

"This is so typical Matt," Lizzie complained as she and Miranda walked down the street. "I mean, I set rules and he breaks them. He doesn't think of the consequences of his actions."

Ruin Dad's football, ruin our lives. Not exactly hard to remember!

Miranda raised her eyebrows. "Sounding a little parental, aren't we?"

"Miranda, you didn't lose your little brother," Lizzie said.

What's this weird feeling i'm having? i'm . . . worried?

"Lanny and Matt are out there all alone and it's my fault," Lizzie went on. She felt the guilt settle in her stomach.

Miranda pulled Lizzie's arm through her own. "It's not all your fault."

"I don't know what I'm going to do if we can't find them." Lizzie pressed her lips together, holding back tears.

"We'll find them," Miranda assured her.

"Well, where do you think they'd go?" Lizzie asked.

Miranda stopped in her tracks and thought for a moment. "Okay, I'm a geek with a popped football signed by some famous guy."

Lizzie looked like she knew exactly what Miranda was saying. "Oh, oh! Collector's Corner, the comic book store!"

Miranda looked skeptical. "Do they sell footballs there?"

"They sell *everything* there!" Lizzie cried. "It's like the geek version of the mall! Come on."

CHAPTER FIVE

Gordo had his feet up on the couch and was sipping a soda. He was watching some big-time Hollywood movie featuring tons of cool explosions when the doorbell rang. "Mmmm . . . pizza," Gordo said as he hauled himself off the couch.

When he opened the door, Gordo found himself face-to-face with two enormous guys in white jerseys with green sleeves. They were the Bleacher Boys, Jeremy and David. They were Mr. McGuire's two best friends from his softball team. When Lizzie had told her mom that Matt and Lanny were "playing quietly," Mr. McGuire had called and asked them to check on the kids.

"So you guys deliver pizza, too, huh?" Gordo asked. For some reason, this didn't surprise him.

"Mmmmm . . ." Jeremy said as he stepped into the foyer, "pizza."

"Nah, Sam called us." David frowned down at Gordo. "We're just here to check up on you guys."

"Oh well, we're all doing great," Gordo said brightly. "Everything's A-OK. So, see you later." He tried to shut the door, but Jeremy stuck out a beefy arm and shoved his way back inside.

"How dumb do you think we are?" Jeremy asked.

Gordo hesitated for a moment. "Do you really want me to answer that?"

David planted his hands at his waist. "We need visual confirmation that everyone's . . ." He grinned at Gordo, then mimicked, ". . . A-OK."

"Everyone's upstairs," Gordo said, thinking quickly. "They'll be down in a second. Yeah, go, uh, make yourselves at home." He escorted the Bleacher Boys to the couch.

My only hope now is to try to distract them with food, Gordo thought. And hope that Lizzie gets home soon!

Matt looked around the Collector's Corner Comic Book and Memorabilia shop. He'd never been inside before, although he'd often peered into the cluttered windows as he walked by. He was surrounded by comic books, collectible posters, trading cards, ancient toys, pinball games, a shelf full of bobble-head dolls, autographed baseballs, jerseys, and basketballs. It was like walking into a treasure trove!

Lanny and Matt stepped up to the counter. On a high shelf was a series of autographed footballs.

"C'mon," Matt said as he scanned the names, "Walter Payton, Walter Payton."

BRETT FAVRE, read the plaque below the first football, JIM BROWN, DICK BUTKUS, JOE MONTANA, DAN MARINO, EMMITT SMITH, WALTER PAYTON . . .

Lanny pointed and Matt's face lit up. "Walter Payton!" Matt cried. A golden aura seemed to shine from the ball—their quest was at an end.

"Can I help you?" sneered a voice.

The nerdy shop owner was standing behind the counter, glowering at them. He had long, unwashed hair, glasses, and was wearing a moldy, brown cardigan. Matt placed the withered football on the counter, and slid it toward the shop owner.

"What is this?" the shop owner asked disdainfully.

"It's an autographed Walter Payton football," Matt explained.

The shop owner looked skeptical. "Perhaps in a former life," he said. Curling his lip, he picked up the football between his forefinger and thumb. "Now it's more like an autographed Walter Payton pancake." He gave a nerdy half-snort, half-laugh.

Matt hesitated. This really wasn't going the way he'd planned. Lanny nudged Matt, so he decided to use a tactic that had worked on countless adults over the years. Trying to look as pitiful as possible, Matt started his story. "Me and Lanny—this is Lanny—"

Lanny waved.

"You see, it's kind of our fault that this football is ruined," Matt said. "It's my dad's, and it's really, really important to him." Lanny looked up at the shop owner with huge eyes. "And if I don't get him a new ball, then I'm in big trouble, and Lanny's in big trouble, and my sister, who really didn't do anything, is going to be in big trouble."

The shop owner nodded. "Sounds like a really touching story. . . ."

Lanny put his hands on Matt's shoulders to show his support.

"So we were hoping maybe that you would exchange this ball for that nice, new one," Matt said pleadingly, pointing to the auto-graphed Walter Payton football that sat high on the shelf.

The shop owner looked over his shoulder at the football. "Hmmm . . . let me think about that."

Matt looked up hopefully, sniffling a little, for added effect.

"No!" the shop owner scoffed.

Matt seemed to deflate, not unlike the squashed football. He let out a series of boohoos. Lanny put his arms around Matt and patted him on the back. The two were still hoping the shop owner would come around, but he walked off, indifferent to Matt's wailing.

"Matt!" cried a voice. "Matt."

It was Lizzie and Miranda. And for once they were happy to see Lizzie's little brother!

Gordo sat on the couch, squeezed between the two enormous Bleacher Boys, who were sipping soda and munching on the pizza he had ordered. Gordo's stomach rumbled. He'd tried to grab a slice of pizza earlier, but Jeremy had batted his hand away. Now he was just hoping that all of the food and soda would make Jeremy and David sleepy, so that he could escape before they'd realized that Lizzie and Matt weren't really upstairs. . . .

David looked around. "I thought you said they'd be right down?" he asked, his mouth full of pizza.

"Yeah. Hey!" Gordo said brightly, changing the subject. "Say, you guys like jokes? I've got a great one." Gordo scanned his memory for a joke. He decided on Old Reliable—the King of Norway joke!

"Okay," he said, standing up and plunging ahead, "so the King of Norway, he goes out into the woods with his, his number one hunter, right? . . ."

"How did you guys find us?" Matt asked.

"Well, we just pretended we were a couple of geeks," Miranda explained, "and where would we be?" Looking up, Miranda realized that the other geeks in the store were looking at her. She winced. "Sorry."

"Matt, what were you thinking, taking off like that?" Lizzie demanded. She held back from telling Matt that she'd been worried sick. That would be way too "Mom."

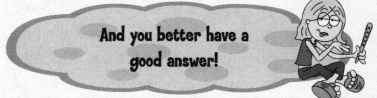

And you better have a good answer!

"Well, we just thought—what would you do in this situation?" Matt told Lizzie as he fiddled with the ruined football. "Well, you wouldn't get into trouble in the first place," he admitted. "But you'd try to fix it."

Oh. That's a pretty good answer.

Grrr! Lizzie thought. Why does Matt have to pick now of all times to be sweet? That is so like him! Now I can't even be mad.

"And that's what we tried to do," Matt finished. Lanny nodded.

"You really scared me," Lizzie admitted.

Matt looked surprised. "I did?"

"Yeah, you did," Lizzie said slowly. Wow, now that my heart is back to beating normally, I realize just how hard it was pounding before! She took a deep breath. "And right now, the football doesn't even matter. All that matters is that you two are okay and we get you guys home safe."

Matt and Lanny smiled.

"You know, I really hate to interrupt this little Hallmark moment," Miranda put in, "but we do have some parents to beat home."

Matt looked down at the football. "That's it," he said miserably. "We're done for."

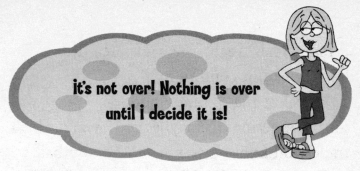

it's not over! Nothing is over until i decide it is!

"No." Lizzie gestured for the ball. "Give me the football."

"What are you doing?" Miranda whispered as Matt handed it over.

"I'm saving the day," Lizzie said coolly as she strode up to the counter. "Excuse me, Mr. Comic Book Guy?"

The shop owner regarded her with a bored expression. "You're wasting your time," the shop owner said. "I already told the little hobbit no."

"Excuse me, sir." Lizzie plowed ahead, ignoring the guy's tone. "I have here an autographed Walter Payton football."

The shop owner did his little snorty-laugh

thing. "Yeah, yeah," he said sarcastically, "in less-than-mint condition."

"I realize that." Lizzie nodded. "But I was just wondering if maybe you would do a trade. You know, give me another football."

"Interesting." The shop owner pursed his lips thoughtfully. "Tell you what, I'll give you a Dick Butkus for a deflated Walter Payton."

Lizzie thought for a moment. Let's see . . . Dick Butkus versus Walter Payton . . . Okay, I have no idea who either of those guys are, so . . . "Deal," Lizzie said quickly.

Miranda's brow furrowed in confusion. "What's a Dick Butkus?" she asked.

"I don't know," Lizzie admitted as she took the ball from the shop owner. "But he's all we got right now. Come on."

Matt, Miranda, and Lanny hurried out of the shop, led by Lizzie, who had the new football tucked under her arm.

I've got the ball and I'm headed for the end zone, Lizzie thought. I just hope I make it home before I get tackled by Mom and Dad!

"It's mine," Jeremy said as he batted David's hand away from the last piece of pizza. Snatching the slice, he shoved it into his mouth.

". . . The King of Norway said . . ." Gordo paused, wanting to give his punch line all of the oomph he could muster. He'd been telling this joke for half an hour, and he knew that it had to pay off big. "'I thought he said he . . .'" Just then, Gordo caught sight of Lizzie and Miranda outside the window. And Matt and Lanny were with them. Gordo opened his eyes wide, and hopped off his chair to distract the Bleacher Boys. "'I thought he said he was a moose!'" Gordo crowed. Glancing out the window toward Lizzie and company, Gordo pointed upstairs.

The Bleacher Boys stared at him blankly.

Lizzie saw the Bleacher Boys waiting in there. She waved frantically, motioning for Gordo to stall them. Then she and the others dashed off.

"That joke was terrible," David said.

"Yeah," Gordo said slowly. "I guess it was. Maybe . . ." Gordo realized that he could stall for another full half an hour if he told the joke all over again. That is, if he could remember the stream of endless babble that had poured from his mouth. Deciding it was worth a shot, Gordo said, "Maybe that's 'cause I told it wrong. Let me start again. How does it go? Okay. So the King of Norway, he goes out into the woods with his number one hunter and—"

Thunk!

The noise had come from upstairs.

"What's going on up there?" Jeremy demanded, frowning at Gordo.

"Nothing?" Gordo said nervously.

Thunk!

"Let's go check it out," David said, as if he were a detective on some bad cop drama. Jeremy flipped the pizza box closed and tossed it on the coffee table as the Bleacher Boys headed for the stairs. Gordo trotted after them, wondering whether it was too late to try to interest them in another joke.

CHAPTER SIX

Lizzie was halfway through the window when Gordo burst into her room ahead of David and Jeremy. Thinking fast, Miranda pulled down the shade to hide her friend. Then she and Lanny crowded in front of Matt, who was hiding the Butkus football under his shirt.

"What's going on up here?" David demanded as he barreled through the door.

Miranda, Matt, Lanny, and Gordo looked up at him innocently.

"Nothing," Miranda said sweetly.

Jeremy counted the kids. "Somebody's missing," he said finally, cocking an eyebrow. "Where's Lizzie?"

From her place half in and half out of the window, Lizzie tried to stay quiet. *I know it's too much to hope for yet another miracle today,* she thought. . . .

Just then, the front door slammed.

"Mom and Dad!" Matt shouted.

"Hello?" Mr. McGuire called. "Anyone home?"

Matt, Lanny, Miranda, and the Bleacher Boys shuffled out of the room to go greet the McGuires. Gordo stayed behind, and once the room was all clear, he turned his attention to Lizzie.

"Help me, help me," Lizzie wailed as

Gordo dragged her through the window.

"You okay?" Gordo asked.

Lizzie rolled her eyes. For now, she thought. I'll be fine until Dad finds Dick Butkus sitting on our mantel!

Miranda and Lanny did their best to cover Matt, who still had the autographed football under his shirt, as they stomped down the stairs, followed by the Bleacher Boys.

"Hey, guys," Mrs. McGuire said with a smile. "Everything okay?"

"Fine," Matt said quickly.

"Great!" Miranda chirped.

Lanny blinked at the McGuires, trying to look as innocent as possible.

Mr. McGuire frowned at the Bleacher Boys. "Where's Lizzie?"

"We can't find her," David admitted.

Mrs. McGuire looked concerned. "What

do you mean, you can't find her?" she asked.

"Yeah," Mr. McGuire echoed as he and his wife exchanged a look. A moment later, they were marching upstairs, the Bleacher Boys behind them.

Lanny stood in front of Matt, hiding the football. The minute the adults headed upstairs, Matt dashed toward the living room to stash the football on the mantel, but his mom was too quick. Reaching out, she grabbed him by the collar. Lizzie was missing, and in Mrs. McGuire's mind there was only one person who could have caused that to happen. . . .

"I'm sure you had something to do with this," she growled, hauling Matt up the stairs. "You're coming with me."

Matt looked scared. But his mom still hadn't seen the football. The minute she turned to go up the stairs, Matt pulled the ball from beneath his shirt and got ready to pass it to Lanny.

"Lanny," Matt whispered.

Matt tossed the ball, and Lanny caught it and hid it behind his back.

This time, there was no interception.

Lizzie walked out of her room just as her parents and the Bleacher Boys reached her door.

"Hey, guys," Lizzie said lightly. "How was the sports thingie?" She gave them a wide smile.

Mr. and Mrs. McGuire stared at each other, as Jeremy and David gaped at Lizzie. They knew she hadn't been in her room before. . . . Well, they thought she hadn't been. . . .

Meanwhile, downstairs, Lanny darted this way and that, evading imaginary tacklers as he rushed toward the goal line—the mantel. Reaching the football stand, Lanny placed the ball carefully in its place, then did a victory dance.

". . . And the high point of the day," Mr. McGuire said later that afternoon as the whole family sat in the kitchen, "was when I got my picture taken with last year's Super Bowl mascot."

Lizzie rolled her eyes. She could just imagine her dad grinning his face off as he stood beside a sorry-looking guy in a donkey suit.

Mr. McGuire walked out of the kitchen.

"So, did you kids do anything fun today?" Mrs. McGuire asked as she sat down at the kitchen table with a snack and a soda.

Fun, Lizzie thought as she took a sip of her soda, hmmm. . . .

Let's see, destroying a football, chasing Matt and Lanny across town, and sneaking back into the house without getting caught. Yeah, it was fun.

"Nah," Lizzie said, sneaking a look at her brother. "We didn't have any fun."

"Just another boring day," Matt chimed in.

Lizzie and Matt shared a secret smile.

"Who would care to explain this to me?" Mr. McGuire asked as he walked into the kitchen carrying the Dick Butkus autographed football.

What was that about fun again? Lizzie thought.

So close, yet still so, so busted.

Lizzie felt the smile drop from her face.

"Explain what?" Mrs. McGuire asked.

"How my Walter Payton signed football has magically become a Dick Butkus signed football?" Mr. McGuire said, his voice rising.

Matt sighed. "It's all my fault," he said miserably.

"No," Lizzie put in quickly, looking up at her parents, "it's all my fault."

Lizzie and her brother looked at each other. "It's our fault," they said.

"We ruined your football, Dad," Lizzie confessed.

Mrs. McGuire plucked the Butkus football from Mr. McGuire's hands. "Is this authentic?" she asked, sounding seriously impressed.

Lizzie shrugged. "Well, the guy at the store said it was."

Mrs. McGuire grinned. "And you traded in dad's ruined football for this?"

"We're really sorry," Matt said sincerely.

Mrs. McGuire chuckled—then let out a real laugh.

Stop laughing! Lizzie thought, glaring at her mother. My life is over—this isn't funny!

"You guys are really good," Mrs. McGuire said, with real admiration in her voice.

Wow—chalk one up under unpredictable, Lizzie thought.

Mom's taking this really well.

"What are you talking about?" Mr. McGuire demanded. "They ruined Payton and brought back a Butkus."

"If I were you guys," Mrs. McGuire went on, ignoring her husband, "I would have just bought another football and signed it."

Giving them a wry grin, she added, "That's what I did."

"You did what?" Mr. McGuire cried.

"Well, the football that Lizzie and Matt ruined was actually a Walter Payton football autographed by Jo McGuire," Lizzie's mother admitted.

Lizzie sat back in surprise, and Matt's jaw dropped.

"The real one accidentally fell into the fireplace a couple of months ago," Mrs. McGuire went on. "Accidentally," she stressed quickly.

Mr. McGuire looked as though he were trying to absorb way too much information for one day. "It did?"

"Yeah," Mrs. McGuire said gently.

"So, technically," Lizzie said carefully, "we didn't ruin Dad's football."

"And we got him a football signed by someone more famous than Mom!" Matt added.

Lizzie's mother laughed.

"So, technically, we can't be grounded, right?" Lizzie asked hopefully.

Mrs. McGuire thought about that for a moment. "Wrong," she said quickly.

I should have known we wouldn't get off that easy! Lizzie thought.

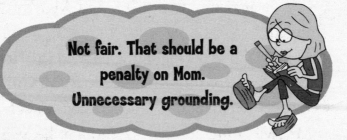

Not fair. That should be a penalty on Mom. Unnecessary grounding.

"Okay," Mr. McGuire said, grabbing the football from his wife, "from now on, this football is off-limits to everyone in this house except me." He stalked off to put his new, authentic Butkus football in its place of honor. Grinning, Mrs. McGuire followed him out.

"You know," Matt said to Lizzie as they both stood up from the table. "I really am sorry for messing up your day. I didn't mean to." He thought for a moment. "Well, yes, I did," he admitted, "but just not that much."

"I know." Lizzie smiled at him. "And I'm sorry for coming at you so hard. I didn't mean to."

"Yeah, you did," Matt said. "But you're my sister and that's your job."

Lizzie laughed. "I know."

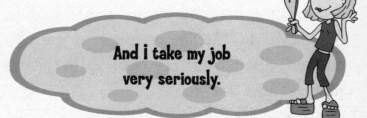

And i take my job very seriously.

But there was something that was still bothering Lizzie. "So," she told her brother, "you do know that if you ever need something, I'm here for you, right?"

Matt smiled wryly. "Yeah."

Reaching out, Lizzie gave him a quick hug. Wow, she thought, it's been a long time since I've done that. Funny—it wasn't actually that bad. Matt could be annoying . . . but he could also be sweet. "Okay," Lizzie said finally. "But if you ever run away like that again," she said, looking Matt straight in the eye, "I'm going to totally crush you."

"I know," Matt said.

Lizzie reached for a pretzel, and Matt grabbed the bowl away, his eyes twinkling mischievously. "Whatcha going to do?" he taunted, darting out the door to the living room. "Come and get it!"

Lizzie took off after him.

Finally, she thought as she raced after him, everything is back to normal.

Don't close the book on Lizzie yet!
Here's a sneak peek at the next
Lizzie McGuire story. . . .

Adapted by Alice Alfonsi

Based on the television series, "Lizzie McGuire", created by Terri Minsky

Based on the episode written by Douglas Tuber & Tim Maile

"**L**isten to me! All of you!" Lizzie McGuire's substitute teacher, Mr. Dig, cried out.

Lizzie and her half-asleep classmates jerked fully upright behind their desks. Whoa, what is up with Mr. Dig? thought Lizzie. Too much coffee at lunch?

Their teacher paced the classroom, then stopped and threw his hands into the air. "Turn off your TVs! Read a book!" he shouted.

Lizzie glanced uneasily at her two best friends. David "Gordo" Gordon didn't seem too fazed by this directive. Miranda Sanchez, however, seemed annoyed. She pursed her lips and raised her hand. "Hey," she stated defensively, "I just read something last week."

"Miss Sanchez," snapped Mr. Dig, "the latest issue of some new fanzine doesn't count."

Miranda winced and shrunk down in her seat.

Whoa, Lizzie thought, Mr. Dig's really got the 411 on this class.

"What about *you*, Mr. Gordon?" the teacher challenged, pointing an accusatory finger at Gordo. "What have you read in the last week?"

"*One Hundred Years of Solitude, On the Road, Seven Pillars of Wisdom,* and *Schnozzola: The Jimmy Durante Story*," Gordo instantly rattled off.

Mr. Dig blinked in surprise at Gordo. "See, I was trying to make the point that you kids don't read enough," he said. "You kind of cut my legs off there."

"Oh," said Gordo with a shrug, "sorry about that."

Note to Mr. Dig, thought Lizzie, here are a few things you *never* want to challenge Gordo on: being well-read, completing his homework, and movie trivia.

"I'm assigning a book report," Mr. Dig stated flatly.

The class groaned.

Why are they groaning? i like reading. . . . *Harry Potter*, *Eloise*, books about cats who solve crimes—it's schoolwork you can do lying down.

"I want all the girls to read *The Orchids and Gumbo Poker Club*," Mr. Dig declared, "which is about mother-daughter relationships and social climbing."

Now it was Lizzie's turn to groan. "Mother-daughter relationships?" she muttered, rolling her eyes.

This is starting to sound like one of those open-and-shut books. i'm going to want to shut it as soon as i open it!

"And I want all the boys to read *A River Runs Through It*," Mr. Dig continued, "which is about father-son relationships and trout."

Gordo nodded happily. He liked trout. "That's g-o-o-d eatin'," he joked.

Lizzie leaned toward Miranda. "I actually like reading," she whispered, "but about mother-daughter relationships? I get enough of that at home."

As far as Lizzie was concerned, her relationship with her mother mostly came down to a few simple daily phrases: "brush your teeth," "clean your room," "get good grades," "clear the table," and the answer "no" to anything related to costing money or acquiring permanent tattoos.

Later that evening, Lizzie went to her room and settled on her bed with *The Orchids and Gumbo Poker Club*. She opened the cover with a heavy sigh, not wanting to read one line, let alone seven whole chapters. But Mr. Dig was going to grade her on a book report, so she forced herself to forge ahead.

Chapter One, Lizzie read to herself. *Defining moments. They come and go in our lives like streetcars and summer breezes. Like the sweet subtle blush on a honeysuckle blossom— here for the most fleeting of instants . . . then gone again. Do we pick these moments? Or do they pick us?*

Lizzie sat up a little straighter. This is actually sort of interesting, she thought. I mean, I can relate, because I'm always thinking about how certain crucial moments will define my own life. Like, what will be the ultimate consequences of my not making the cheerleading squad? Or deciding to quit rhythmic gymnastics? Or tripping over a garbage can in front of Ethan Craft?

Lizzie continued reading *Orchids,* and by

the end of chapter one, she was completely hooked. The story was about a young woman named Darcy Lou, who lived on the Louisiana bayou with her mother, Tallulah. Darcy Lou and her mother were poor, but they were very close, so when Darcy Lou fell in love with a wealthy boy from a prominent New Orleans family, her mother vowed to do everything in her power to make Darcy's dream come true.

"*Darcy Lou quietly removed her gloves, set them on the divan, and blew out the candle,*" Lizzie whispered after a solid hour of reading. "*After that, there was only night and stars and the memory of love.* End of chapter five."

Lizzie swallowed. She hadn't expected the book to be such a tearjerker. *Mr. Dig should have warned us to have a box of tissues nearby,* she thought before bursting into waves of sentimental weeping.

"It's so beautiful!" Lizzie cried. "She's so sad! She loves her mom!"

That's so beautiful!

Sorry! That's the end of the sneak peek for now. But don't go nuclear! To read the rest, all you have to do is look for the next title in the Lizzie McGuire series—

THE 'RENTS

A COMEDY SERIES
THAT'S AHEAD OF ITS TIME

PHIL OF THE FUTURE→

Disney CHANNEL
ORIGINAL

WEEKENDS AT 7PM|6C
DISNEYCHANNEL.COM